THE CELLAR DWELLERS

WRITTEN AND ILLUSTRATED BY THOM HALL

THE CELLAR DWELLERS

You know the dark spot in the corner of the cellar?

The small crack in the wall?

The wet spots from the leaky pipes?

That is where we live. You can't see us though, we are really tiny but we are there.

We are The Cellar Dwellers.

I am Darg,

the biggest of The Cellar Dwellers.

Roller doesn't count because she

likes to raise her hands above her

head and say she's the biggest...

I am.

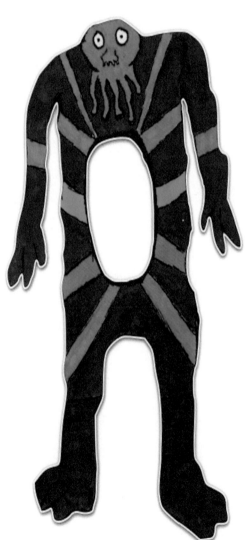

ROLLER

Quiet Darg! We all know the truth.

Anyway, I'm Roller. Having eight arms

sure makes it easy to roll everywhere.

I guess that's why they call me Roller.

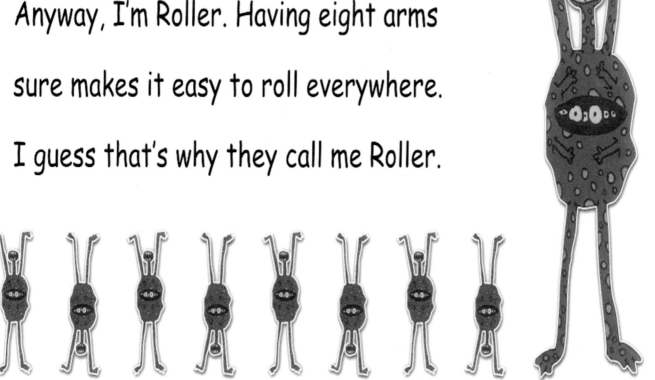

I am Plarp...   and I am Darp...

We come from the same mold
spot under the washing
machine. Our friend Eye
comes from there too but he
is not like us.

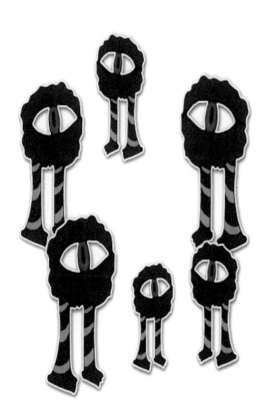

We are Eye. There is

really just one of me,

but I can multiply myself.

I have Eyes everywhere.

SORB

I am not of this world. I came here long ago to observe the beings on this planet. It turns out that I was not big enough to be with the humans and now I am stuck with these Cellar Dwellers.

I'm Leafly. They called me that because one day some leaves blew into the cellar and I came flying in with them. So, leaf plus fly equals Leafly.

LEAFLY

SLUGGER

My good friend, Dono, found me slugging around the cellar sink one day. I can fit anywhere, the smallest crack to the tiniest pipe! It really helps that I don't have any bones.

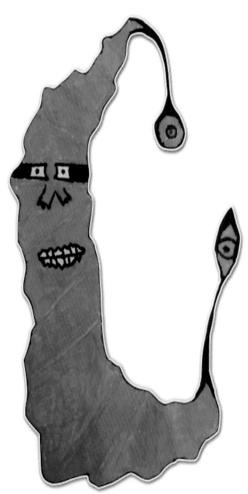

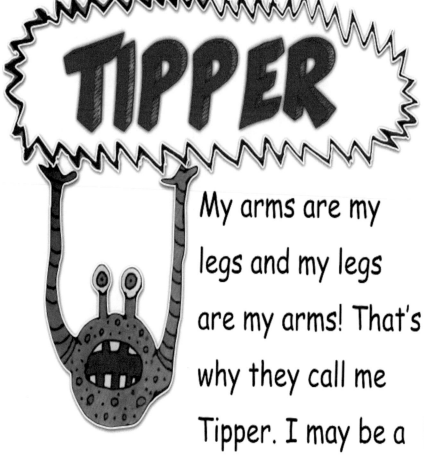

My arms are my legs and my legs are my arms! That's why they call me Tipper. I may be a little off balance but I can climb anything.

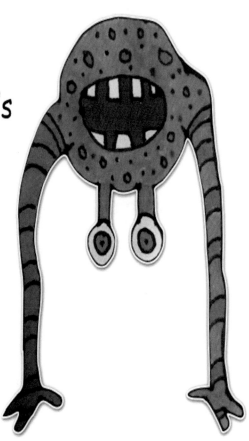

Someone must have dropped some donut crumbs in the cellar. If they didn't I wouldn't be here. Zip found me one day while he was zipping around.

He asked, "Are you a donut?" I said, "don't know." Now I'm Dono.

ZIP

I'm fast, like super fast!

I'm so fast that you can't

even see me move. I was

the first Dweller and from all

of my zipping around I found

most of the others.

Remember that time no one could find any sponges? Well, I'm whats left of them. The name's Suds!

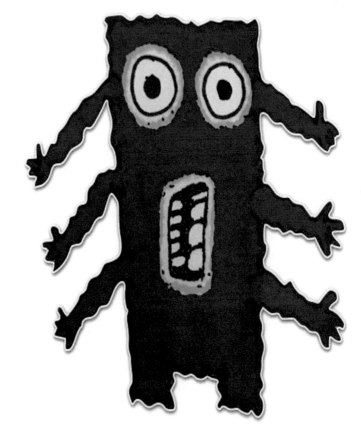

ZIG AND INKY

I'm Zee. My best friend is Inky down there. I always get worried about Ig eating him, but I wouldn't ever let that happen. Ga would rather be left out of this but it is not like he has a choice, being our third head and all.

We are all different, but at the end of the day we are all the same.

We are friends and would do anything for one another.

We are The Cellar Dwellers.

The Cellar Dwellers will return in...

THE ADVENTURES OF THE CELLAR DWELLERS

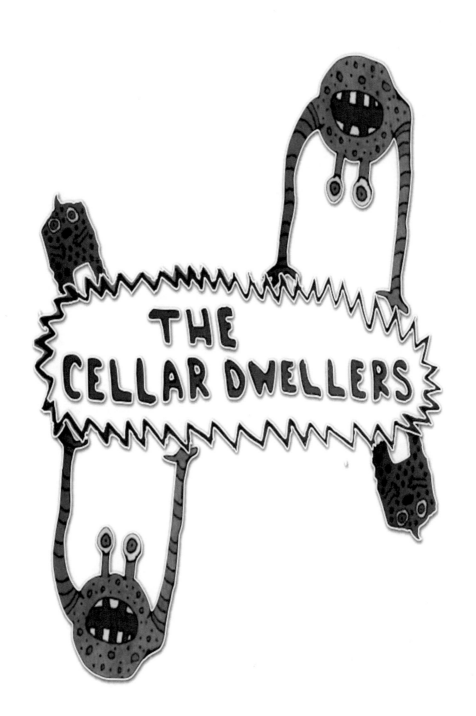

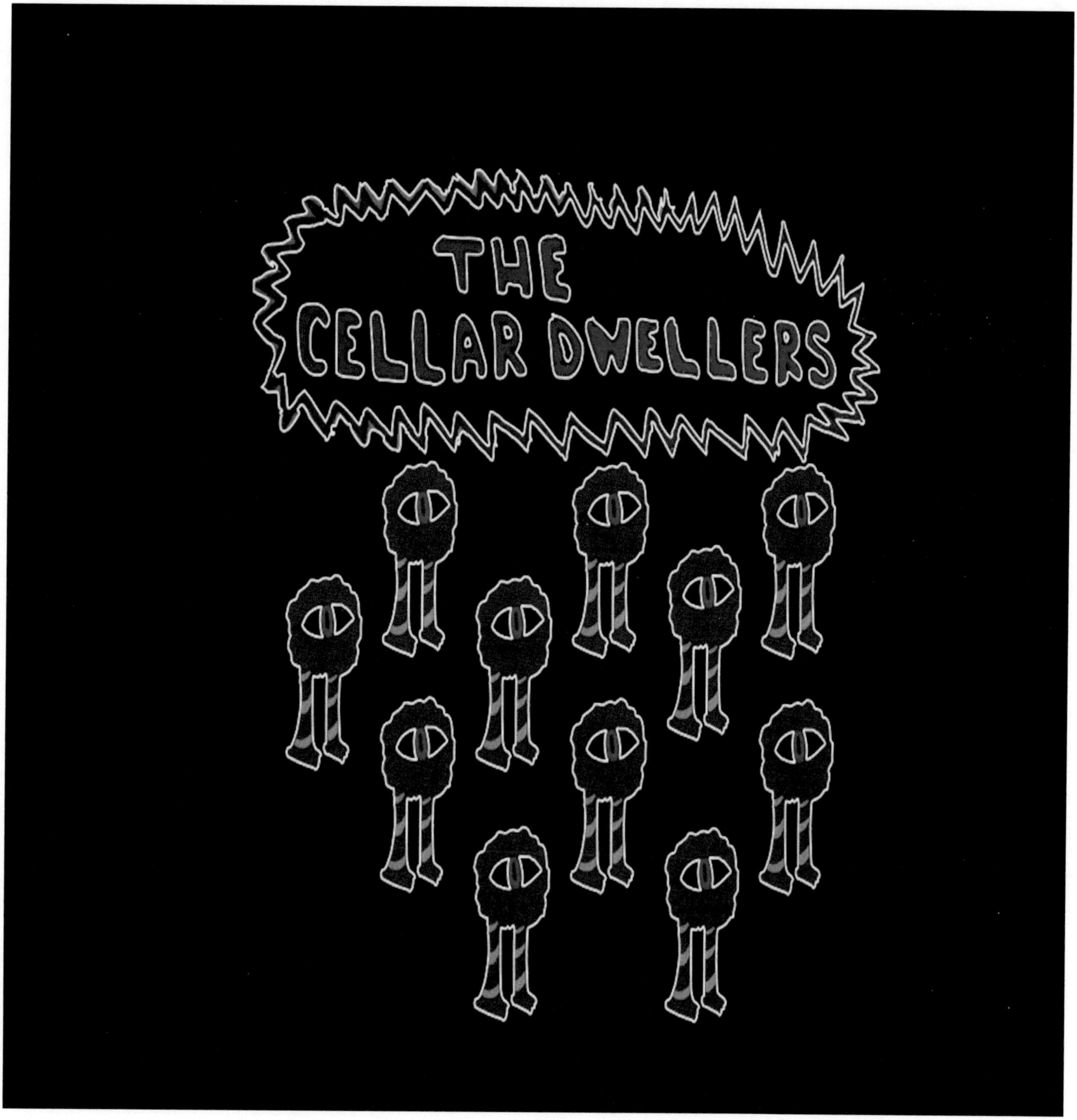
THE
CELLAR DWELLERS

THE CELLAR DWELLERS

ISBN: 9781091597952 (Paperback)

Written and Illustrated by Thom Hall

Made in the USA
Middletown, DE
12 April 2019